Fashion Fairy Princess

Bluebell

❀ in Dream Mountain ❀

POPPY COLLINS

■ SCHOLASTIC

Fashion Fairy
Princess

With fairy big thanks to Catherine Coe

First published in the UK in 2014 by Scholastic Children's Books
An imprint of Scholastic Ltd
Euston House, 24 Eversholt Street
London, NW1 1DB, UK
Registered office: Westfield Road, Southam, Warwickshire, CV47 0RA
SCHOLASTIC and associated logos are trademarks and/or registered
trademarks of Scholastic Inc.

ISBN 978 1407 13954 8

A CIP catalogue record for this book is available from the British Library

Printed and bound by CPI Group (UK) Ltd, Croydon, CR0 4YY
Papers used by Scholastic Children's Books are made from wood grown in
sustainable forests.

1 3 5 7 9 10 8 6 4 2

This is a work of fiction. Names, characters, places, incidents and dialogues are
products of the author's imagination or are used fictitiously. Any resemblance to
actual people, living or dead, events or locales is entirely coincidental.

www.scholastic.co.uk
www.fashionfairyprincess.co.uk

Welcome to the world of the
fashion fairy princesses! Join Bluebell
and friends on their magical adventures
in fairyland.

They can't wait to visit

Dream Mountain!

Can you?

✿ Chapter 1 ✿

Rosa fluttered into
Bluebell's sky-blue
bedroom, grinning.
"Guess what's just
arrived!" she cried,
rushing over to where
Bluebell sat on her
enormous four-poster bed.

Bluebell had been doodling fashion designs, but she quickly pushed her sketchpad to one side. She looked up at her friend. "Oooh, is it my new blue silk beret? That was quick. I only ordered it yesterday!"

"No, but this is much more exciting," Rosa said with a shake of her long dark hair. "Look!" Rosa held out a peacock feather inscribed with gold:

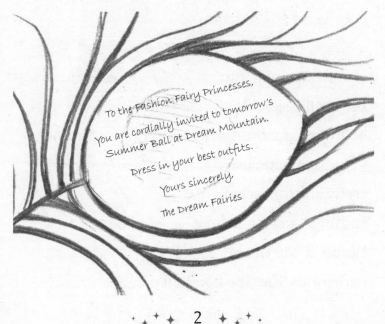

To the Fashion Fairy Princesses,

You are cordially invited to tomorrow's Summer Ball at Dream Mountain.

Dress in your best outfits.

Yours sincerely,

The Dream Fairies

"The Summer Ball!" said Bluebell. "We've never been before!" She bounced on her bed in excitement, then leapt up and grabbed Rosa by the hand. "Quick!" she cried. "Let's go and tell the others!"

Delicately fluttering their wings, Rosa and Bluebell flew along the white marble hallway and into Buttercup's wing of the fairy palace. Buttercup and Violet put down the cupcakes they'd been eating as they read the invitation.

"I can't believe it," Buttercup said quietly, holding up the feather to her yellow stained-glass window.

Violet peered over Buttercup's shoulder. "Is it really tomorrow?" she said, scanning the words once more.

"And we have to wear our best outfits!" Buttercup added.

All four fashion fairy princesses crowded

round the invitation. "Oh my goodness," said Rosa, "we don't have long to prepare!"

The fairy princesses lived in Sparkle City. It was half a day's journey to Dream Mountain from there. They'd have to leave at noon tomorrow to get to the ball in time.

Bluebell reached for a lemon cupcake from Buttercup's sun-painted cake stand. The creamy lemon icing melted in her mouth. Cupcakes always helped calm her down. "So," she began, "what in fairyland shall we wear?"

The four best friends fell silent for a moment. It was a very good question. They had to look their best for the ball.

"We can wear our new diamond-heart tiaras," suggested Violet, ducking into Buttercup's fly-in wardrobe. "The ones Fern made us." Fern was one of their best friends, although she didn't live in Sparkle City, but nearby, in Star Valley.

"But we don't have any ball gowns," said Buttercup. "What will we do?"

Rosa put her arms around her three friends. "We'll go shopping, of course! If we hurry, we'll get to Topaz's shop before it shuts." And in the blink of an eye, the four fairy princesses had fluttered out of Buttercup's bedroom and flown down the grand glass staircase of Glimmershine Palace.

Bluebell, Violet, Rosa and Buttercup arrived at Sparkle Sensations just in time.

"You're in luck – I was about to close," said the owner, Topaz, as they flew through the door to the clothes shop. "What are you looking for, fairy princesses?"

"Those!" all four friends shouted at the same time. They were pointing at the four beautiful sparkling ball gowns that were displayed on mannequins in the shop window. The dresses were identical, apart from the colour. The bottom of each ball gown had tiers of shimmering fabric, with a satin bow in the middle and a halter-neck top covered in gems. What's more, the dresses were in blue, pink, yellow and purple – perfectly matching each of the fairies' wings!

"I ordered them in especially for you," said Topaz. "I'm so glad you like them!"

The fairy princesses quickly changed into the dresses and fluttered around the huge shop. Sparkle Sensations was filled with skirts, dresses, tops, trousers and shoes in every single colour of the rainbow, and the whole shop shone with gems and pearls. It was one of the fairy princesses' favourite places.

Bluebell flew back and forth in front of the floor-to-ceiling mirror. Sparkles danced from her dress as she moved. She was so excited she couldn't keep still! Now they had the perfect outfits for the Summer Ball. Except. . .

"Shoes!" said Rosa, spinning round in her pale pink dress. "We need some to match!"

"Oh yes," said Buttercup, putting a hand to her mouth. She looked down at her golden-yellow ball gown. "I don't think I have any to go with this dress."

Topaz held up a finger covered in glittering rings. "I have just the thing," she said. Topaz fluttered behind a glass door at the back of the shop. She reappeared carrying a teetering pile of boxes. The fairy princesses quickly flew over and each grabbed one before they fell.

Bluebell lifted the lid of her box and her heart leapt. Inside, nestled between layers of delicate tissue, were sparkling peep-toe shoes covered in tiny blue gems. They were gorgeous, and like nothing she'd ever worn before – and they fitted perfectly, too.

The four fashion fairy princesses stood in front of the mirror in their completed outfits, beaming from ear to ear. Violet did a little pirouette in her deep purple dress, surrounding her friends with sparkles. "Now we're ready for the ball!" she said.

Yes, they were – and Bluebell couldn't wait!

Chapter 2

The next morning, the fairies were rushing around the palace, getting ready for the ball. The palace was frantic – like a beehive, Bluebell thought, with everyone fluttering about madly. The fairy princesses had decided to travel to Dream Mountain by horse and carriage – they didn't want to tire themselves before the party by flying all the way. One of the hummingbirds had delivered another message from the dream fairies earlier that day, saying they could change into their ball gowns once they'd arrived at Dream Mountain. The fairy princesses were relieved – they didn't want to ruin their new outfits by travelling in them on the long journey.

Bluebell was almost ready – just one last fingernail to paint in the powder-blue varnish she'd chosen to match her dress. "Come on, it's time to go!" she heard someone call from outside. Bluebell peeked out of her star-shaped window and looked down. Rosa was outside the fairy palace, waiting on the cobbled pathway. Bluebell blew on her fingernails and jumped up from her shiny blue mussel-shell dressing table.

Bluebell's mouth gaped open when she fluttered out of the glittering fairy-palace

doors. In the driveway stood the most
incredible carriage she'd ever seen. It was
made of pink frosted glass, and the doors
were draped with shimmering white silk.
The four lilac ponies pulling the carriage
neighed in greeting.

Bluebell spotted Buttercup stroking each
pony's muzzle in turn. Buttercup seemed
to have a special connection with any
animal she met. *It's because she's so gentle,*
thought Bluebell.

Rosa and Violet poked their heads out from the carriage. "Let's go!" cried Violet, who had a pretty purple flower in her long curly hair.

"Coming!" cried Bluebell. She leapt in, with Buttercup right behind her. Bluebell fell on to the red velvet cushions inside. They felt as soft as candyfloss.

The ponies moved off gracefully and the fairy princesses sat back to enjoy the ride. Another carriage followed behind them, carrying their dresses and accessories. It gave off sparkles as it went. *It must be because of our magical dresses,* thought Bluebell happily. She couldn't wait to put on her outfit!

The fashion fairy princesses journeyed along the silver cobbled paths of Sparkle City. They passed all sorts of fairies on their way. "There's Ruby," said Violet, waving to her fairy friend, who was fluttering into the doorway of Jewels and Gems. It was a jewellery shop that the fairy princesses loved almost as much as Sparkle Sensations.

Before long, they'd left the paths of the city. The ponies were flying from cloud to cloud on their way to Dream Mountain, flapping their wings powerfully. "Isn't it magical?" Bluebell said, peering out of the carriage window. The sky around them was alight with rainbows, and shooting stars darted high above.

"Look!" cried Rosa. She was staring out of the front of the carriage. "Dream Mountain!"

Straight ahead, a mountain loomed up from behind a huge, pink-tinged cloud. Wispy silver mist surrounded it on all sides, and Bluebell could just about make

out the white-tipped peak – but she had
to crane her neck to do so.

The ponies slowed their beating wings,
descending gracefully towards the base
of the magical mountain. As they landed
gently, two dream fairies glided out to
greet them.

"Welcome to Dream Mountain,"
said one, who wore a flowing lilac sari
embroidered with gold thread. "I'm Lily."

"And I'm Snowdrop," said the other
fairy. She had the most gorgeous waist-
length silvery-white hair that was tucked
behind her little ears.

The four friends jumped out of their
carriage and beamed at the dream fairies.
"We're the fashion fairy princesses," said
Violet. "We're so happy to be here!"

Lily smiled and beckoned them to a
tiny gap in the mountain. "Please come
into our home," she said. "We'll show you
to your dressing room, where you can
prepare for the ball."

All four fairy princesses squeezed
through the slit in the mountainside and
then gasped. Inside was an enormous cave
that glittered with fairy dust in every

corner. Shining silver stalactites grew down from the high ceiling like hundreds of pointy fingers. Glossy stone steps rose up from the sides of the cave, and at almost every step was a glitter-edged doorway, leading off to somewhere else in the mountain. Lily and Snowdrop took the staircase to the far left, which was adorned with lanterns to guide the way.

"We're lucky to have a huge home here," said Snowdrop in a delicate, lilting voice. "There's lots of space for guests."

"We can't wait for the ball to start," added Lily as she fluttered up the steps. "Here we are!"

They'd stopped at an arched doorway, and Bluebell peeked in. "Oh, it's beautiful!" she said. The large room was lit by tea lights set into shelves in the cave, and the walls sparkled as the lights flickered. There were four pearl dressing tables, and four silk-covered stools. Bluebell couldn't help but jump when more fairies seemed to burst out of the walls! But then she realized her mistake. One side of the cave was in fact a great glass mirror.

"We need to go and put some finishing touches to the ballroom decorations," said Snowdrop. "The Dream Queen is attending the ball, and she doesn't often come down from her castle at the top of the mountain. We want everything to be extra special!"

"Yes, we'll leave you to get ready," said Lily gently. "Ah, here's Frederick with your luggage."

A smart elf dressed in a top hat and tails appeared. He was carefully balancing all of the fashion fairy princesses' dress bags, cases and shoeboxes as he climbed the stone steps of the cave.

He set them down in the dressing room, bowed to the fairy princesses and then rushed out behind the dream fairies. Bluebell guessed he was very busy today!

"I can't wait to get ready," said Rosa. "Let's start right away – we don't want to be late!"

But Bluebell was only half listening. She'd opened one of the boxes to admire her gorgeous new shoes, but all she had found was tissue. She took the second box from the pile – but that was also empty.

"What's wrong?" asked Buttercup, frowning.

Violet had already rushed over and was flinging the lids off the remaining two boxes. But they were empty too!

"Oh no!" cried Bluebell. "Whatever's happened to our beautiful new ball shoes?"

❋ Chapter 3 ❋

"Maybe Frederick already set them out for us downstairs?" Rosa suggested.

Buttercup nodded. "Of course — that must be what's happened," she said in her soft voice.

Bluebell felt a wave of warm relief wash over her. "Thank fairy for that!" she cried. She fluttered down on one of the stools and began combing her hair with the hairbrush set out on the dressing table. It was made of pearl, with the softest unicorn-hair bristles. The trip here had been wonderful, but Bluebell's short brown hair had been blown around so much it felt like she had a million knots to tease out.

Violet was repinning the flower in her hair, while Buttercup helped Rosa restyle her long dark hair into a beautiful French plait, threaded with pink ribbons.

"I wonder what the ball will be like?" mused Rosa. "Do you think we'll be dancing all night?"

Bluebell jumped up and spun on the spot. "I think there'll be dancing, and lots of delicious food – ooh, and maybe even some musicians in a live band." She pretended to play the trumpet, skipping around the dressing room and tooting and hooting, and soon all four fairy princesses were in fits of giggles.

"With you around, Bluebell, we'll definitely have fun, whatever happens!" laughed Violet, sitting back down on her stool and staring into the mirror, "I wonder if any of our other fairy friends will be here. Do you think Fern has been invited?"

"That would be wonderful!" said Buttercup as she pinned up the sides of her wispy blonde hair in tiny twists. "We haven't seen her for ages."

"I'm not sure," said Rosa, who was admiring her French plait in the giant mirror on one side of the room. "Fern would have had to travel even further than us to get here. But it would be lovely if she does come – and I bet she'd wear one of her gorgeous handmade dresses."

"I wish I could make my own clothes," said Bluebell. "But every time I try, I drop needles everywhere!"

"Can you imagine how many beautiful dresses will be on show at the ball?"

murmured Buttercup. "I can't wait to see all the fairies together."

"I suppose we should hurry up and finish getting ready," said Rosa, jumping up from one of the pearl-encrusted dressing tables, her wings fluttering nervously. "Otherwise we won't see any of the dresses, or the fairies, or the ball!"

Violet had already wandered over to where their tiara cases had been placed on the floor. "Here, let's put on our tiaras first, to check they go with our hair, and then we can put on our dresses."

Even the tiara boxes were covered in glitter. They sparkled in the candlelight as Violet gathered them in her arms. She gave the blue-glittered box to Bluebell, the pink-glittered box to Rosa, and the golden-yellow glittering box to Buttercup, keeping the purple one for herself.

Bluebell was just adding some diamante butterfly clips to her hair, but she stopped when she realized the other three fairies had gone strangely silent. She swung round from her dressing table mirror, and saw all her friends staring into their tiara cases.

"It's not here!" Rosa cried.

Bluebell quickly grabbed her sparkling case from the table and, taking a deep breath, opened it. She gulped – hers had gone missing too!

"This can't be a coincidence, not with the shoes as well," said Violet. "Who's taken our things?"

"Wait – we don't know they've been taken," Buttercup said quietly. "Maybe we forgot to pack them."

Rosa was shaking her head, making her plait swing from side to side. "No, we definitely brought them – I checked the carriage three times!"

"Well, as long as we've got our ball gowns, it doesn't really matter," said Bluebell, trying to look on the bright side. "I'm sure we can ask the dream fairies if we can borrow some tiaras. Let's put our dresses on – that'll make us feel a lot better!"

The fashion fairy princesses all perked up at this. They were *so* looking forward to wearing their beautiful ball gowns. Bluebell skipped over to the open wardrobe where their dress bags were hanging. She lifted out the blue one, and felt a tingle of excitement as she pulled down the zip – she always loved wearing new clothes, but she'd never been this excited about putting on a new dress before. She stuck a hand in the bag to take out the hanger, but it felt light. *Too* light. She felt around, her heart racing with panic, but there was no dress inside!

Tears pricked Bluebell's eyes as she turned to face her friends. "M-m-my dress," she stammered. "It's disappeared!"

"What?!" Rosa rushed over to the wardrobe and pulled out her own dress bag.

"It can't have. They were definitely all there this morning!"

But it was true. All the dresses, along with the matching accessories, had vanished. The four friends stood staring at the empty dress bags, feeling hollow with disappointment.

"What's happened — where have they gone?" said Buttercup, a deep frown lining her pretty forehead.

"I don't know," replied Violet, her brown eyes narrowed in concern. "But this isn't just a case of us mislaying things — something bad is going on, I'm sure of it!"

Chapter 4

Buttercup frowned at the empty boxes and bags. "Let's not panic," she said. "I'm sure there's an explanation for this."

"But Rosa crossed everything off on a list before we left," cried Violet, "so how could they have all gone missing?" She shook her head sadly.

"Please don't worry," said Bluebell. "I'm sure we'll find them — especially since the dresses give off sparkles everywhere they go."

"You're right," Rosa nodded. "Let's start by asking the dream fairies if they know where our things are."

The four friends rushed out of their dressing room and flew down the stone steps of the dream fairies' cave. They bumped into Snowdrop at the bottom, carrying a stack of cake boxes balanced under her chin.

"Snowdrop, have you seen our belongings?" Violet asked her breathlessly. "They've all disappeared!"

Snowdrop frowned, her green eyes turning serious. "They're not in your room?" she asked. "I thought Frederick had delivered everything there."

Buttercup shook her head. "Our boxes and bags were all empty," she explained. "But we're really sorry to bother you — I'm sure you've got lots to do without worrying about us. They must be around here somewhere."

"Yes, please don't worry," added Rosa as Snowdrop's frown grew deeper. "But if it's OK with you, we'd like to search Dream Mountain to try and find them."

"Of course," said Snowdrop. "Please go ahead. Perhaps check the carriage park as well as inside the cave? Maybe they got left behind there. It's around the other side of the mountain – go out of the main entrance and follow the path to the right. And I'll ask the other dream fairies in case anyone else has seen them."

"Thanks, Snowdrop," said Bluebell, "that's a really good idea. Violet, Buttercup, perhaps you could have a look in the carriage park, and Rosa and I will search inside?" She fluttered her wings nervously, desperate to track down their outfits and put an end to their panic. This wasn't how their first Summer Ball was meant to be!

"Of course!" said Violet, taking Buttercup's hand and flying out of the cave door. "Sorry!" she called as she bumped past guests trying to get into the ball. "But this is a fashion emergency!" At that moment, Bluebell was secretly pleased that Violet could sometimes be quite pushy!

"Good luck!" Rosa called after them.

Bluebell and Rosa quickly began to flutter up one of the sets of stone steps in the huge hallway, both of them keeping their eyes peeled for any sign of their clothes.

"What's that?" Bluebell pointed to an elf who had emerged from a door right at the top of the same staircase. In his hand were bundles of fabric in different colours. Could it be their dresses?

Rosa squinted in the candlelight. "I'm not sure it's our things. I can't see any sparkles," she said. "And why would that elf have them?"

But Bluebell had already zoomed up towards the little elf, her pale blue wings fluttering so hard they were a blur. "Stop! Wait!" she called after him.

By the time Rosa had caught up with Bluebell, the elf was shaking his head and turning into the next doorway along.

"It wasn't our outfits," said Bluebell in a small, disappointed voice. "Just some satin bed linen he was putting out for guests. Sorry."

"Don't worry," said Rosa. "There are still plenty of places to search." She turned around and pointed across the other side of the cave. "How about that corridor there – it looks like lots more dressing rooms."

"Good plan," said Bluebell, and she took the lead, skimming just below the beautiful gleaming stalactites as she flew across the cave hall.

As the two friends landed on the glossy staircase opposite, three smiling fairies zoomed out of one of the doorways nearby. But when they saw the fairy princesses' faces, they stopped abruptly and their grins vanished.

"Are you OK?" asked one of the fairies, who was dressed in a peach ball gown trimmed with tiny amber gems.

"Not really," admitted Bluebell. "We want to get ready for the ball, but all our outfits have gone missing. They're halterneck ball gowns in pink, yellow, purple and blue. I don't suppose you've seen them?"

The three fairies shook their heads. "I'm really sorry," said one with short black glossy hair clipped at the side with a bright red rose. "But you could try the other rooms up here. We'll keep a look out for them too," she offered.

"Thanks," Rosa replied. "That would be great."

The two fairy princesses continued along the corridor, asking every fairy they met whether they'd seen any of their belongings. But no one had, and Bluebell and Rosa were running out of rooms to check and fairies to ask. What's more, it was much quieter now – most of the fairies had finished getting ready and had left for the ballroom.

Bluebell felt sick with worry. "If we don't find our outfits soon," she said, slumping down on the stone staircase, "we're going to have to miss the ball!"

Chapter 5

Rosa put an arm around her fairy friend. "Come on, we can't give up yet. Anyway, perhaps Violet and Buttercup have found the outfits in the carriage park."

Bluebell felt a glimmer of hope. "Shall we go and find them?" she suggested.

Rosa nodded. "I think we've searched as much as we can in here."

The two fairy princesses flew down

one of the staircases, passing the kitchens on their way. Bluebell glanced in – it was full of elves and fairies stirring and cutting and baking. The smells wafting out of the doorway were delicious – fruity and sweet, savoury and spicy. Bluebell hated the thought that they might miss out on all these tasty delights!

Bluebell and Rosa made it back to the entrance, where hundreds of fairies were flying through the doors. Most of these later arrivals were already dressed in their ball outfits, and they all looked stunning. Bluebell spotted a fairy wearing a particularly gorgeous turquoise dress with a train held up by dragonflies. The outfit looked like it would be so much fun to dance in! Another fairy was wearing an ice-white lace dress with a long scalloped hem. Over her head was a delicate white veil spun from cobwebs, and her necklace had the biggest pearls Bluebell had ever seen. *They must have come from Glitter Ocean,* thought Bluebell, but there was no time to stop and ask.

"Look, there's Buttercup and Violet," said Rosa, pointing to the other side of the large cave doorway.

Bluebell's heart fluttered with hope as she spotted Buttercup's silky blonde hair. *Have they found our precious outfits?* she wondered.

But as they flew over to join them, she saw their hands were empty.

Violet and Buttercup were shaking their heads. "We're sorry," said Buttercup, "we looked EVERYWHERE in the carriage park, but we couldn't find any of our missing things."

"We didn't just search inside our carriage, we looked underneath it too!" added Violet as she brushed off dirt and dust from her purple denim jeans.

"We lifted the cushions, and even looked under the seats – I thought that maybe our things had somehow been squeezed into the little gaps there," Buttercup explained. "But there was nothing – not even any sparkles to give us a clue."

"How about you?" asked Violet. "Did you find anything inside the cave?"

Rosa shook her head sadly. "Nothing – and the cave's becoming so crowded that it's getting harder and harder to look."

"You're right – it looks like almost everyone has arrived," said Buttercup, her blue eyes wide with worry. "The Summer Ball must be starting very soon!"

"I think we're going to have to go home," said Bluebell. She had a lump in her throat as she tried really hard not to cry.

The fashion fairy princesses looked distraught. They were so disappointed to be missing the ball.

"Let's go back to our dressing room to collect our things," said Rosa. "We'll just get more miserable if we stand about here."

They fluttered sadly up the stone steps of the cave, passing fairies in ball gowns coming the other way. They tried to smile bravely at the excited fairies who were on their way to the ballroom.

"Wait, what's that?" Bluebell's eye had been caught by something flickering out of one of the dressing-room windows just a little way up. She was sure it was sparkles! Could it be the trail of their dresses? The fairy princess rushed into the room, her pale blue wings fluttering. She peered out of the small triangular window cut into the cave wall. The window didn't let in much light, as it looked out over the misty landscape of Dream Mountain. But there – she was certain she could see glints of sparkle through the magical fog!

All four fairy princesses were at the window now, staring hard at the bumpy, grass-covered mountainside.

"Come on!" shouted Violet, already flying back to the door of the dressing room, her hands up in the air. "What are you waiting for?"

Chapter 6

Moments later, the fairy princesses were fluttering nervously up the steep and misty mountainside — all except Violet, who whizzed ahead. *She doesn't seem at all worried about exploring*, thought Bluebell. But she was a bit concerned about the foggy mountain — it looked like it'd be easy to get lost out here. She turned to Buttercup and Rosa. Their faces showed how she felt – tight with concern, lips pursed together and eyes wide.

The fairy princesses could see the sparkles up ahead, twinkling in the mist between two large, moss-covered rocks.

"It's a cave entrance!" Violet said, zooming quickly inside.

"Do you really think we should go in there?" Rosa called quietly to Violet, but the purple-winged fairy had already disappeared.

Bluebell peered into the opening in the mountainside – Violet was right, it was another cave, with beautiful stalactites hanging from the top and crystal fossils set into the sides. It didn't look especially scary, but they didn't know Dream Mountain at all, and Bluebell wasn't sure that they should be going deeper into the mountain.

Even Buttercup, who loved nature, hesitated. "I'm sure it's fine," she said, but her voice didn't sound very confident.

"Hey, hey!" came a noise which seemed to echo in the cave. Where was it coming from?

Bluebell spun round, her heart racing. What was it? She couldn't see anything through the mist that surrounded the mountain.

Then two figures began to take shape.

"It's OK!" one of them called. "It's only us – the dream fairies. We've come to help you."

Bluebell almost collapsed with relief.

"We saw you climbing up here when we were directing carriages to the carriage park," said the dream fairy on the left, who wore a dark green full-length sari with a beautiful neckline decorated with tiny glass beads.

"We were about to go inside to the ball," explained the other dream fairy, who had auburn hair and wore a gorgeous satin dress. "But we knew something must be wrong when we spotted you. Can we help?"

Bluebell gave them as big a smile as she could muster. "We're looking for our lost outfits," she explained. "We saw sparkles leading into the cave, so we think they might be here."

By now, Violet had flown back to the others. "What's happening?" she panted, out of breath, and then she spotted the dream fairies. "Oh, thank fairyland you're here – you'll help us, won't you? We don't know our way around the caves but we really need to find our dresses!"

Bluebell hoped Violet's bluntness hadn't offended the dream fairies, but they only smiled.

"Of course – we were just saying so,"

said the auburn-haired one. "I'm Iris, by the way."

"And I'm Jasmine," said the fairy in green.

"Our outfits are very special," explained Rosa, "and give off sparkles everywhere they go. We thought that'd make it easy for us to track them down – but we've only spotted seen this clue, and we've been searching all day!"

Iris put an arm around Rosa. "Please don't worry – if they're somewhere on the mountain, then we promise we'll find them."

"And it isn't as scary as it looks," said Jasmine. "Follow us, we'll show you."

With Iris and Jasmine guiding the way through the cavernous tunnels, the fairy princesses felt much less frightened. They ducked and leapt, fluttered and swirled. The further into the mountain they went

the colder it became, and Bluebell rubbed
her arms to keep warm as she fluttered
her blue wings behind Iris. The sparkles
were in sight now – four distinct trails of
yellow, pink, purple and blue. *They* must
be from our outfits! thought Bluebell.

Jasmine was beckoning them all on from
the front of the group. "If you're careful
not to disturb anything in the mountain,"
she whispered, "then the mountain will be
kind to you in return."

Now that Bluebell's eyes were adjusting to the darkness, she saw how beautiful her surroundings were. The cave's fossil-covered walls glistened, and brightly coloured moss sprang up from the rocky floor, like a blanket for the ground. She saw pretty purple dragonflies darting above her, and bright blue fireflies dancing down on webs from the stalactites.

"It's incredible, isn't it?" Buttercup mouthed to Bluebell as they fluttered past a deep blue pool filled with little green fish. Bluebell turned to look at the water, just for a second, and almost flew into Rosa, who had come to an abrupt halt behind the dream fairies.

"The sparkles!" whispered Rosa. "They've gone!"

Bluebell had been so distracted by the beauty of the cave that she hadn't noticed straight away, but, sure enough, the multicoloured sparkles they'd been following had disappeared. Iris and Jasmine were still zooming in and out of the cave tunnels, trying to find the trail again. But it was nowhere to be seen, and the fairy princesses shook their heads silently, as if to give up.

Bluebell's heart sank into her shoes. That was it, then – they'd never find their outfits now. They'd have to go home, and miss their first ever Summer Ball. She let herself drift slowly to the ground, but as she landed she stumbled backwards, tripping over a group of silver stalagmites that grew up from the cave floor behind her.

"Are you OK?" asked Buttercup, fluttering down, her hand outstretched to help her friend up.

But Bluebell didn't reply, because from the floor she could see what they'd all missed before now. Not just the sparkles, but their entire outfits, nestled on a ledge at the very top of the cave!

Chapter 7

"There they are!" Violet shouted as she followed Bluebell's gaze. But Jasmine was shaking her head while pulling Violet away from the ledge.

"Stay quiet," Iris hissed. "Your clothes aren't just stuck there — it looks like they're being used as a nest!"

Sure enough, when they looked closely, the fairy princesses could make out a few tiny beaks poking out of the sparkling fabrics.

"They're golden dream eagles," Jasmine said softly. "Of course — they love anything that glitters. The mother eagle must have seen the trail of sparkles from your dresses when your carriage arrived."

"The golden dream eagle is a very rare bird that lives in Dream Mountain," Iris explained. "Its feathers are made of gold and they contain special magic that prevents bad dreams."

"Wow," murmured Buttercup, her eyes alight with wonder. "They're beautiful."

Bluebell could see the mother eagle now, her wings shimmering with a bright golden sheen. The majestic bird was hovering at the edge of the nest, delicately feeding her young as they reached up to her beak.

"Should I fly up to the ledge and try to ease our things out of the nest?" suggested Violet.

Bluebell sucked in a breath — it was just like Violet to offer to do something so daring!

Iris shook her head. "No, we can't do that," she said. "The golden dream eagle and her chicks should never be disturbed. If they want to communicate, it is up to them to approach us."

Jasmine's face was creased with concern. "Because of the magic they carry, we have to be very careful around them. We really should leave them in peace in the cave."

"But without our clothes, we can't go to the ball!" said Violet. She turned round, away from the other fairies. Bluebell could tell that her friend was very upset, but she didn't go after her — she know Violet preferred to be left alone when she was feeling down.

"At least we found out what happened to our outfits," said Bluebell quietly. "And it's not as if the eagle meant any harm. She didn't know what she was taking."

All six fairies flew slowly back through the vast tunnels, away from the nest of the golden dream eagle. Bluebell now felt more confident in navigating the dark cave, but she felt sick with disappointment that they wouldn't be going to the ball. Everyone was very quiet — even Violet.

Bluebell rubbed her eyes as she flew out of the cave entrance, suddenly exhausted after such an eventful day. Then she rubbed them again, and blinked. She could see a narrow trail of golden mist, quite different from the white mist that surrounded the mountain.

"Iris, Jasmine," Bluebell called gently but urgently. The dream fairies at the front of the pack spun round. "Have you seen this before?" The fairy princess pointed up towards the mountain summit – there was definitely a trail of something up there, and it seemed to be getting closer!

The dream fairies both looked up, their eyes wide. "No, that's very strange indeed – and the trail seems to be coming from higher up the mountain," said Iris.

"Should we follow it?" asked Rosa.

"Please?" added Violet. "I know it's not our outfits, but it could be important."

By now, the trail had got so close, Bluebell could almost reach out and touch the golden mist. Where – or who – was it coming from?

"I think you're right, Violet," said Bluebell, and then she turned to the dream fairies. "Iris, Jasmine, we don't want you to miss out on the ball too – we'll be fine on our own, I promise."

"If you're sure?" said Jasmine.

Bluebell nodded. As the gorgeous golden mist swirled around the four fashion fairy princesses, she had a feeling it was meant just for them.

"All right, then." Iris was pulling
Jasmine's hand, her face already alight
with excitement about the ball. "Good
luck, and we hope to see you again soon."

As the two pretty fairies left, Bluebell
felt a stab of sadness. She wished she
could see them later at the ball. But her
three friends were already making their
way up the mountainside – she had no
time to wallow in her disappointment.
"Wait for me," she called softly, flapping
her light blue wings to take off towards
them.

As they climbed higher, the swirls of mist got thicker — as if they were in the middle of a giant fluffy cloud.

"Wow," said Buttercup, her mouth gaping open. "This is incredible."

"Do you think we're safe up here?" Rosa asked, looking around her.

But the thick mist cloud didn't look dangerous to Bluebell — just very magical.

"Look, the golden trail's heading even further upwards," Violet pointed out, and all four fairies continued on their way, barely able to see each other through the fog, the wetness settling on their skin like talcum powder.

As they flew, it felt as if the trail of golden mist had the power to pull them ever closer — as if they had no choice but to follow it as it continued to wrap itself around all four fairies. When Bluebell reached out to touch it, if felt like popping candy glittering and bursting on her fingers.

Suddenly, the mist-cloud cleared, as if blown away by a giant gust of wind. At last, the fairies could see what lay in front of them, and Bluebell staggered forward at the view. They were at the very peak of Dream Mountain, and before them stood a delicate, small but beautiful ice-white castle, the sun bouncing off it, making it sparkle like a giant crystal.

"My fairyness!" cried Rosa. "It must be the Dream Queen's palace!"

The grand white stone door of the palace began to open slowly, and Bluebell held her breath. As the door opened fully, a serious-looking elf appeared in the centre. "The Dream Queen says to come in, quickly, please!"

The fairy princesses looked at one another in horror – were they in some kind of trouble? There was only one way to find out. . .

Chapter 8

Violet led the way to the Dream Queen's castle door, but even she looked nervous, Bluebell thought.

The elf pulled the stone door open wider to allow them to enter, and bowed as he did so. Inside, every white wall, floor and surface glistened — as if it were ice — but when Bluebell brushed against the wall it was surprisingly warm to the touch. It felt like a very special place.

The short elf led the fairy princesses along the main hallway to one of the rooms at the rear of the palace. He kept silent as they moved – giving no clue as to what the Dream Queen wanted with them.

They got to the very end of the hallway, to a grand marble door flanked by two marble fairy statuettes. The elf stood on his tiptoes and knocked gently.

"Come in," came a deep, echoing voice from inside. The elf pushed open the door and hurried the fairy princesses inside — still without saying a word.

Bluebell looked down at herself and her heart fluttered with panic — they were meeting the Dream Queen looking like they had been through a firefly storm backwards!

Inside, the Dream Queen's parlour was huge. Unlike the rest of the palace, it was decorated in all the colours of the rainbow — with splashes of red, pink, purple, blue and yellow across the walls — and when the fairy princesses glanced down, they saw the floor was made of tiny gold mosaic pieces. Bluebell couldn't help but smile — she loved colours, and this was so wonderful after the stark white of the palace outside.

The Dream Queen sat on a golden throne at the far end of the parlour, in front of a mirrored wall, which showed the nervous reflections of the fairy princesses. The queen had waves of golden hair, and wore a black velvet cape threaded with multicoloured silk.

"Hello, fairy princesses," said the queen. Her voice was low but smooth, as if she could send them off into a beautiful sleep at any moment.

"I'm so sorry we look like this," Bluebell began. "We've had a rather disastrous day."

"Please don't worry — I know all about it."

"You do?" said Violet. "But how?"

The queen smiled at the question. "I know about everything that happens here. Not only that, but as the Dream Queen I also grant wishes to fairies in need. And it sounds as if you lovely fairy princesses are very much in need."

Bluebell was relieved they didn't have to explain everything that had happened. Was she really going to help them too?

"Now close your eyes," the queen continued, "and no peeking."

The four friends squeezed their eyes tightly shut. Bluebell shivered as she felt a gentle breeze flick about her shoulders.

"Now you can open them," said the queen.

As the fairy princesses widened their eyes again, the Dream Queen was lowering a long, diamond-tipped wand. Then they all sighed with joy and amazement as they caught a glimpse of themselves in the mirror. They were dressed in beautiful ball gowns – the ones they had lost! What's more, their feet twinkled in their new peep-toe shoes, and nestled in their hair were the diamond-heart tiaras.

Rosa began to curtsey, nudging the others to do the same. "I don't know how to thank you, Your Majesty," she said.

"You don't need to," the queen replied. "All the thanks I need is for you to enjoy the Summer Ball. Now let's go, before you miss the first dance!" She stood up, towering over the fairy princesses. "Close your eyes again," she murmured.

The air swirled around them once more. Bluebell felt herself lifting up and slowly spinning, but she dared not open her eyes, not even a slit. Suddenly, her ears were filled with the most tuneful tinkling of music she'd ever heard.

"Now open!" called the Dream Queen.

The four friends couldn't help but squeal with delight when they saw where they were. They stood on a shiny black stone stage, and in front of them was a

magnificent ballroom – easily as big as
their entire fairy castle back in Sparkle
City. Fairies fluttered everywhere, all
wearing gorgeous ball gowns in every
colour and fabric imaginable.

There was Lily, wearing a netted lilac tutu and silver tights, and Snowdrop, who had on a stunning long red dress that made her look like a poppy flower. They spotted Iris and Jasmine, wearing gorgeous golden tassel-edged saris, who both beamed with happiness at the sight of the fairy princesses at the ball after all. Bluebell felt weak at the knees at the beauty of it all, and grabbed on to Buttercup before she fell over.

"Isn't it amazing," the blonde fairy whispered. "Look, there's even a dragonfly band."

Bluebell looked up in the direction Buttercup's tilted head. A dozen tiny dragonflies were flying around the ceiling, making music by darting in and out of little silver harps.

The Dream Queen broke Bluebell's daze. "Before you go and enjoy the ball, I have something else for you," she said.

Bluebell looked down at the Dream Queen's outstretched hands and gasped. In them were four golden feathers. Could they be. . . ?

"These are fallen feathers from a golden dream eagle," the queen confirmed. "I want you to have them as a souvenir of your visit here, and I hope they help to make up for the tricky day you've had."

"Thank you!" the four friends breathed as the Dream Queen passed a feather to each of them. It felt soft and magical in Bluebell's hand.

"Now have fun, fairy princesses," she said, and gave a small wave of her hand.

As the princesses flew down from the stage, sparkles dancing behind them, Violet pointed out the decorations. The stone walls were covered in tiny glow-worms, lighting up the room with a magical greeny-yellow light. And the room was edged with glass tables that held sparkling drinks, dainty sandwiches and melt-in-the-mouth iced cakes.

Just then, the dragonfly harpists went quiet, and the Dream Queen's voice boomed out from the stage. "It's almost time for the first dance of this year's Summer Ball," she began. "The dream fairies and I hope you all have a wonderful time."

As soon as she finished speaking, several elves appeared on the stage, carrying different horn instruments. They stood, nodded at one another, and began to play. It was the kind of fast, fun music that you couldn't help but dance to, and soon every single fairy in the ballroom was tapping her feet and flapping her wings. The fashion fairy princesses' dresses billowed gently as they danced, the layers floating up and down like clouds.

As Bluebell twirled Buttercup around, grinning with delight, she felt a tap on her shoulder. She spun round.

"Fern!" she cried. Her dark-haired friend was dressed in an emerald green maxi-dress with sequinned green ballet pumps to match. Bluebell gave Fern a huge hug. "We hoped you'd be here!"

Soon all five friends were joined in a group embrace, smiling and jumping to the music. Despite their difficult day, the Summer Ball was turning out to be everything the fashion fairy princesses had hoped for, Bluebell thought, as she pirouetted into the centre of the group, making everybody laugh. All their troubles had been worth it, and now she wished that the ball would never end!

If you enjoyed this

Fashion Fairy Princess

book then why not visit our
magical new website!

- ✿ Explore the enchanted world of
  the fashion fairy princesses
- ✿ Find out which fairy princess
  you are
- ✿ Download sparkly screensavers
- ✿ Make your own tiara
- ✿ Colour in your own picture frame
  and much more!

fashionfairyprincess.co.uk

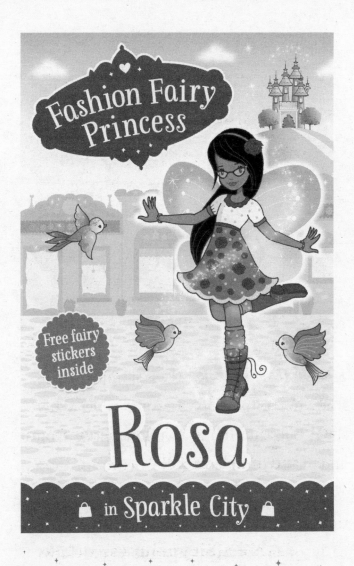

Fashion Fairy Princess

Free fairy stickers inside

Rosa

🛍 in Sparkle City 🛍

Turn the page for a sneak peek of the next Fashion Fairy Princess adventure...

Chapter 1

KNOCK KNOCK! Rosa jumped up from her pink glass dressing table, where she'd been combing her long dark hair, and fluttered over to the bedroom door. Who could it be? She guessed it was one of her three best friends, but it was early on a Saturday morning, and Rosa was almost always the first fashion fairy princess to wake up.

She twisted the rose-shaped doorknob and slowly opened the door.

"Good morning, Princess Rosa," said a tiny double-winged fairy-helper who stood in the palace corridor. "Your presence is required in the Royal Hall. Please hurry — the king and queen are waiting for you." With that, the dainty fairy flew off to her next errand, her wings fluttering so fast she became just a blur.

Rosa's mouth dropped open in surprise — why did the fairy king and queen want to see her? But there was no time to worry about that! The fairy princess quickly changed from her pink cloud-cotton nightgown into a fuchsia bell skirt and a strawberry-print top. She hoped it was smart enough for the fairy king and queen. They lived in a separate wing of Glimmershine

Palace, which they didn't leave very often, as the king was old and rather frail. It meant the fairy princesses rarely saw them, so Rosa knew this must be something important. She pulled her long hair into a high ponytail, slipped on her favourite walnut-wedge shoes and added her dark-rimmed glasses to complete her look – then she rushed out to the hallway.

"Rosa! We were just coming to get you!" said Bluebell. The fashion fairy princess was fluttering in the corridor next to Rosa's two other best friends, Buttercup and Violet.

"Did you get the message?" asked Violet, her brown eyes bright with excitement.

Rosa nodded. "Yes!" she replied. "We'd better hurry!"

One after the other, the four fashion fairy princesses flew as quickly as they could along the white marble hallway. They fluttered down the sweeping glass staircase without putting so much as a foot on a step. At the bottom of the stairs, they spun round in the diamond-tiled entrance hall and then sped off along the ground-floor corridor to the right. This led to the king and queen's wing of Glimmershine Palace, past walls that were filled with magical mirror-glassed portraits of all the past fairy kings and queens. When she was little, Rosa spent hours in this hallway just looking at the beautiful pictures. She secretly hoped she might become the fairy queen one day.

The corridor began to widen, and the fairy princesses soon saw a huge arched golden door, guarded by a tall, golden-

feathered cockerel. "Cock-a-doodle-doo!"
it cried in a loud, ringing voice.

Rosa looked round at her three friends.
She suddenly felt very nervous!

Fortunately, nothing seemed to scare
Violet. She had already stepped forward,
pushing the heavy golden door with
one hand. The other fashion fairy
princesses shuffled along behind her,
letting out gasps as they took in the
Royal Hall. They'd been there before, on
very special occasions, but the room still
took their breath away. It was enormous,
with a sparkling glass domed roof. The
bright fairyland sunshine that poured
through it made everything in the hall
glisten – especially the jewel-covered
walls and polished-silver-stone floor.

Along both the right and left walls stood
the cutest pink fairy-bunnies Rosa had

ever seen, each with miniature wings and holding tiny trumpets. She noticed that at the end of the Royal Hall, the two ruby thrones were empty. The fairy princesses waited, not daring to move a muscle.

Suddenly, the fairy-bunnies brought their trumpets to their mouths. They chorused a short rising melody that was both beautiful and important-sounding. The four friends grabbed each other's hands tightly, and as the bunnies lowered their trumpets, in came the fairy king and queen through an arch at the back of the hall...

Get creative with the fashion fairy princesses in these magical sticker-activity books!

And coming soon...